Duck for a Day

Duck for a Day

Meg McKinlay

illustrated by **Leila Rudge**

CANDLEWICK PRESS

Text copyright © 2010 by Meg McKinlay
Illustrations copyright © 2010 by Leila Rudge

First U.S. edition 2012

Library of Congress Cataloging-in-Publication Data

McKinlay, Meg.
Duck for a day / Meg McKinlay ; illustrated by Leila Rudge. —1st U.S. ed.
p.   cm.
Summary: When Abby's class gets a pet duck named Max, she is eager to take it home overnight, especially since her parents will not let her have a pet.
ISBN 978-0-7636-5784-0
[1. Ducks as pets—Fiction. 2. Schools—Fiction.
3. Lost and found possessions—Fiction.]   I. Rudge, Leila, ill. II. Title.
PZ7.M4786782Du 2012
[Fic]—dc23   2011018608

11 12 13 14 15 16 BVG 10 9 8 7 6 5 4 3 2 1

Printed in Berryville, VA, U.S.A.

This book was typeset in Stemple Schneidler.
The illustrations were done in pencil.

Candlewick Press
99 Dover Street
Somerville, Massachusetts 02144

visit us at www.candlewick.com

For Sienna, who would surely get the duck
M. M.

For my favorite TOE
Love, L. R.

The Bag That Quacked

Abby leaned forward and stared.

The new teacher's bag was moving.

Abby peered closer. What did teachers have in their bags? Books, probably. And colored markers. Maybe an electric pencil sharpener. But none of those things could move.

At least Abby hoped not.

If an electric pencil sharpener was fighting its way out of that bag, she didn't want to be in the way when it escaped.

Abby looked over at the teacher. She didn't seem to have noticed the bag. She was writing her name on the board in curly purple letters:

Mrs. Melvino

Next to Abby, Lianna was staring at the bag, too. "Hey!" she whispered. "Maybe it's one of those little dogs!"

Oh. Abby hoped not. She had seen those dogs, the kind people carried around in handbags, with little pink bows on their heads.

Last year, Melanie had thought it was cute to bring her poodle puppy in her backpack for show-and-tell.

Abby sighed. If she had a dog, she would never put it in a bag.

She didn't have a dog, though. Because Mom and Dad said no. They said no every single birthday and every single Christmas.

They said no to dogs and cats and rabbits. They even said no to goldfish. Because it was important to keep the house tidy and calm, and pets weren't good at that. Because dogs chewed newspapers, and cats clawed curtains, and even a bowl of goldfish was too messy when you really thought about it, with the water slopping everywhere and the smelly fish food, not to mention how their googly eyes staring at you and their endless swimming around and around would start to drive you crazy before long.

That's what Mom said, anyway.

Abby looked at Mrs. Melvino. She didn't look like a dog-in-a-bag kind of person. She didn't look like the kind of person who would be driven crazy by goldfish swimming around, at least not very quickly.

Mrs. Melvino didn't look like any teacher Abby had ever seen. She had wild, curly hair and rectangular glasses with purple frames. She was wearing a long, flowing skirt with funny little bells hanging off of it, and dangly earrings that jingled when she moved, like the wind chimes Mom hung up out back.

She looked like the kind of teacher who wouldn't mind if you suddenly asked why her bag was moving.

So Abby did.

"My bag? Oh dear, yes." Mrs. Melvino raised her eyebrows. "Of course, it's not really a *bag*."

Abby looked closer. She was right. It wasn't a bag at all. It was a spotted cloth, draped over something.

A cage.

She could see now,
because the cloth was
coming off. Because
something was nibbling
and tugging and pulling at
it from inside.

Something with a smooth, orange beak.

Something with speckled brown feathers.

"QUACK!"

Abby jumped.

Melanie squealed. "What *is* that?"

No one replied. Because anyone could see what the cage thing was. It wasn't a little dog or an escaping electric pencil sharpener. And that was a relief.

But it was weird, all the same.

Because it was a duck.

A duck that was ruffling its feathers and staring out at them with bright, beady eyes as if to say, *What are* you *looking at?*

Not That Kind of Pet

"This is Max," said Mrs. Melvino. "Our class duck."

She reached down and unlatched the front of the cage. Then she clicked her tongue and tilted her head to one side, giving the duck a kind of sideways look.

The duck bobbed up and down as if he was nodding. He poked his head out, looking up and down and all around. Then he put out one webbed foot, fluffed up his feathers, and started waddling slowly across the room.

"Class *duck*?" Melanie pulled her feet up onto her chair. "You can't have a class *duck*."

Mrs. Melvino peered at Melanie over her glasses, a twinkle in her eye. "Really? Well, what would you prefer—a hippopotamus, perhaps?" She looked around the room. "We'd have to knock out a few walls, of course." Melanie giggled. "A duck is probably more sensible, don't you think?" Mrs. Melvino raised an eyebrow. Then she took a metal tub out from under her desk.

She set it up on a sheet of plastic at the back of the room and handed out cups and buckets and ice-cream containers.

"Water!" she said, waving toward the faucet outside.

The class filled the tub. When the duck got in, water overflowed, sloshing down the sides onto the plastic, then out onto the carpet, where it left dark, damp patches.

Abby waited for Mrs. Melvino to freak out and run to grab a towel.

Instead, she smiled and jingled her earrings like wind chimes. "It's only water," she said. "It will dry."

It did.

Then Max wet it again.

And again.

All morning as Abby tried to do her work, Max splashed and flapped and waddled around. He rattled the handle of the craft cupboard. He roamed under chairs and around tables. Sometimes he stopped to pull a shoelace or nibble pencil shavings. Sometimes he nudged gently at the back of legs. Sometimes he nestled his feathery bottom down onto someone's shoes and curled up on their feet.

When he sat on Abby's feet during art, she stayed perfectly still. She didn't get up to go to the bathroom or get a drink or sharpen her red pencil at the electric pencil sharpener.

She had to color half her volcano green, but she didn't mind. She liked the way her feet felt all soft and warm with feathery breathing.

"Excellent volcano!" said Mrs. Melvino. "Very creative."

During spelling, Dale tried to get Max to come to his desk. "Here, Max!" he said. "Here, ducky-duck-duck."

"Oh dear, no." Mrs. Melvino frowned. "Max will not come if you call him. He is not that kind of pet. Not at all."

Then she clicked her tongue and gave the duck another sideways look, and he gave a loud QUACK and waddled away.

Abby sat very still and didn't call him. Maybe that way, he would come back to her.

Noah wanted the duck, too. Abby could see

him trying to click his tongue quietly so no one would notice.

Then Noah did something else.

He put his hand up.

Abby stared. Everybody stared. Because Noah never put his hand up. If a teacher asked him a question, he just mumbled and stared at his desk.

But now his hand was up, and he was calling out a question. And it was a question that made Abby's skin tingle, the way it did when something good was just around the corner.

"Mrs. Melvino," asked Noah, "if Max is our class duck . . . does that mean we can take him home?"

Abby caught her breath.

Because Noah was right.

Because class pets were allowed to come home if your parents said yes. And Abby's parents had said yes.

They had said yes to class pets because they had said no to everything else.

Because the good thing about class pets was they were temporary. They were only for a day or two.

You could clean up their mess really quickly so no one noticed. You could send them back to school, then tidy your house all perfectly, like they were never even there. Then your mom could relax on the sofa with a nice cup of tea and not have to worry about their googly eyes driving her crazy.

That meant you got to have a kind-of-
sort-of pretend pet for a day.

You got to feed it and stroke
it and bounce it softly on the
trampoline.

Abby frowned. Last year
the rabbit didn't really
enjoy the bouncing. It
just sat there quivering
until she put it back in
its cage.

Max seemed different,
though. He seemed like the
kind of pet you could actually
do things with.

He seemed like fun.

Abby looked at Mrs. Melvino
and held her breath.

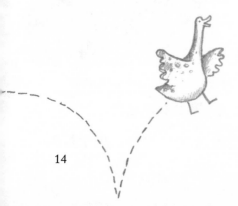

The Duck Has Demands

"Ah," said Mrs. Melvino. "What an interesting question."

Gracie shot her hand up. "Last year we took turns with the rabbit. Only it wasn't really fair because it was alphabetical and—"

"*Turns?*" Mrs. Melvino leaped out of her chair. "Good heavens! There will be no *turns*. There will be no *alphabetical*." She shook her head, making her curls bounce like springs. "Max is not a *rabbit* or a *guinea pig*. He is not some fluffy pet who sits around like a lump. Not just *anyone* can have a duck. A duck is *different*. A duck has demands."

She hurried to the whiteboard and wrote underneath her curly name:

1. No dogs or cats

"That includes neighborhood cats that wander through your yard, even though it isn't really your fault, and you swear you'll watch him every second of every day without even taking any bathroom breaks."

Dale shot his hand up, but Mrs. Melvino ignored him and kept writing:

1A. No ferrets or other clawed or toothy animals of any kind

Dale frowned and put his hand down again.

2. Calm, secure yard

"You must have a fence. With a gate. With a bolt. A bolt that cannot be easily opened by a very clever duck with a very clever beak."

3. Duck food

"Pellets, mostly. Although Max does enjoy the occasional strawberry."

4. Aquatic environment

"Water! So Max can wash and swim and feel at home."

"QUACK!" said Max, flapping his wings wildly.

Mrs. Melvino smiled at Noah. "So, the answer to your most interesting question is . . . most certainly and definitely and without a doubt YES! You may take Max home if you can meet his demands. It is as simple as that."

Abby looked up at the board.

Aquat-ic. The sounds popped like tiny bubbles on her tongue.

She looked over at the overflowing metal tub.

She looked down at Max, at his bright, clear eyes. She felt the nudging of his smooth, clever beak as he pulled gently at her shoelaces.

"*Simple,*" she whispered.

Aquatic Whatever

"A class *duck*?" Mom turned white. "You can't have a class *duck*!"

"Really?" Abby raised her eyebrows. "Well, what would you prefer—a hippopotamus?"

Mom sighed. "Well, only for one night. And no, you may *not* use my laundry tub for your . . . aquatic whatever."

"Okay." Abby shrugged. She didn't need the laundry tub. She already had a plan.

Out back, she dragged her old clamshell swimming pool from behind the shed. She opened it up and brushed off the family of beetles that was living inside. Then she went and got the hose.

As water splashed down onto the hard green plastic, she looked around at the yard.

It was calm.

There were no dogs or cats.

There were no clawed or toothy animals of any kind, unless you counted Noah, who lived on the other side of the back fence and had kind of pointy teeth.

It was secure, too. Unless you counted Noah being able to see in from the tree in the corner of his yard. He was always sitting up there, all creepy and quiet, staring down at her until she got annoyed and went inside.

Somehow, Abby didn't think staring would bother Max, though.

He would probably stare back until Noah got annoyed and went inside.

That would be good, actually.

Then Abby would be able to lie on her trampoline and look for shapes in the clouds without Noah watching her all the time.

It was her special spot back here. At least it was before Noah came along. It was quiet and relaxing and . . .

Thunk. Thunk.

Abby jumped.

Thunk. Thunk.

It was the sound of digging.

Coming from just over the fence.

She climbed onto the trampoline and peered over.

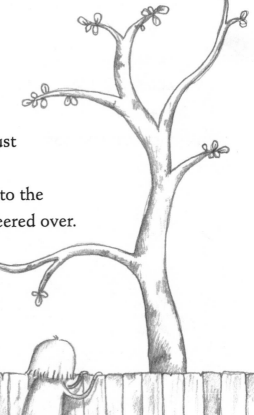

It was Noah. He was just on the other side with his back to the fence. He was digging a hole in the ground with a shovel. Next to him was a hose, with water dribbling out of the nozzle.

"I know you're there," he said suddenly, without turning around.

It was like he had eyes in the back of his head.

Abby shivered. Noah was weird like that, always staring and mumbling, creeping everybody out.

Even the way he came to school was weird. He didn't come at the start of the school year, the way new kids normally do. He didn't even come at the start of the *day*. He just appeared in the doorway with his four sisters, asking where they should put their dirty bags and their chewed-up pencils.

Abby stared at Noah's yard. It wasn't like her place, all neat and tidy. It was an old, falling-down kind of place with a rusty swing set and a hundred lost tennis balls in the long grass.

Dad said they would clean it up after they moved in, but they didn't. Instead, they let the grass grow longer and added more piles of junk.

"You won't get Max,"
Abby said suddenly.

"What?"

"It's not *aquatic*." Abby pointed
down at Noah's hole. "It's just muddy."

It wasn't calm, either, but she didn't
say that.

She didn't need to. Noah knew it wasn't
calm. Everybody in the neighborhood knew
that. There was always noise and yelling
and little kids squealing. That's probably
why Noah was always hiding up in the tree,
halfway into her yard.

And why he kept asking if he could come
over when they first moved in.

He kept asking for weeks, even though
Abby never said yes. She knew she couldn't
say yes even if she wanted to, which she
didn't. She knew Mom wouldn't like Noah,
with his dirty clothes and his messy hair.

Noah shrugged. "Whatever." And he kept
on digging.

Abby dropped back down onto the trampoline.

She looked around the yard again at the clamshell with its cool, clean water. It looked *secure* and *calm*. It looked *aquatic*.

She could see Max splashing around in there already, her very own kind-of-sort-of pet duck for a day.

She flopped onto her back and stared up at the clouds.

She could hardly wait.

The Duck Is Different

"Oh dear, no."

Mrs. Melvino shook her head.

"No swimming pools. The chemicals are not good for Max's feathers."

"No baths. Max likes to be outside."

"No trash cans filled with water. Max is not a piece of *rubbish*."

"No poodles, even if you put them in your bag." She frowned at Melanie. *"Especially* if you put them in your bag."

Abby jiggled on the balls of her feet as she waited. She hadn't thought there would be so many kids, all ahead of her, all trying to get Max.

At least she was ahead of Noah. He was never early. He was always running through

the door after the bell with his shoelaces
undone and his backpack spilling open and
disgusting toast crumbs stuck to the corner of
his mouth.

Finally, it was her turn.

She told Mrs. Melvino about the clamshell
and the cool, clear water. "No chemicals. And
it's outside."

But Mrs. Melvino shook her head. "Oh dear,
no. It's too temporary."

"Too what?"

"Temporary." Mrs.
Melvino smiled. "It
shouldn't be something
on top of the grass. It
needs to be . . ."

"Built-in." It was
Noah, coming through
the door. Abby stared.
He wasn't early, but
he wasn't late either.
"Dug-in."

Mrs. Melvino nodded. "Yes, exactly."

"But the tub isn't built-in."

Mrs. Melvino tutted. "Well, yes, but that's for during the day. For overnight, Max needs something more *permanent,* something more . . . natural."

"But—" Abby began.

"No *buts.*" Mrs. Melvino wagged her finger. "I did tell you. Max is not a furry lump. He is difficult. I mean *different.* Max is different." She looked past Abby. "Now, Noah—are you next?"

Noah explained about his hole.

"It's built-in," he said.

"Very natural," said Mrs. Melvino. "Nice and *permanent.* But it sounds a little too . . . muddy."

Abby smiled to herself.

"A little mud is all right," said Mrs. Melvino. "Ducks enjoy a good mud bath every now and then. But you must have a proper pond, too. A proper, clean, built-in aquatic environment."

"But how can it be clean,"
asked Noah, "if it's built-in?"

Mrs. Melvino twirled one
dangly earring. "Yes, it's quite a
challenge, isn't it?"

Back at her desk, Abby
thought about what Mrs. Melvino had said.

Built-in, but not *muddy.*

Natural, not *temporary.*

She thought about Noah's big muddy hole.

She thought about her green plastic
clamshell.

Then she smiled.

Of course.

Built-in, Dug-in

Every day Abby dug her hole.

She dug up rocks and wood and pieces of junk. When she hit a knot of roots, she sighed and started again, away from the tree.

When she hit some pipes, she sighed and started again, away from the sprinklers.

When Mrs. Melvino decided Noah's mud bath idea was so extremely excellent, she didn't know why she hadn't thought of it herself and added 4A. Mud bath to the list of demands.

Abby sighed and started digging a second
hole, next to the first.

Luckily, her clamshell was split into two
halves. That's what made it a clamshell. That's
what made it perfect for a very demanding
duck who needed a clean aquatic environment
with a mud bath on the side. So she could dig
her holes, all deep and wide, then take her
clamshell and slide it right inside.

"I don't know why you're copying me. It's
too muddy, remember?"

Abby jumped. Noah was up in the tree,
lying on the long branch that stuck out into
her yard.

She glared up at him. It wasn't fair that he was in her yard. But when she told him to get out, he always said, "I'm not in your yard. I'm in my tree."

Technically, he was right about the tree.

She knew he'd been in her yard, though, for real.

Sometimes, when she got home from swimming or gymnastics, she found the trampoline bouncing a little.

At first she told herself it was the wind.

Then she felt the warm patch, right in the middle, like someone had been sitting there.

Or maybe lying on their back, looking up at the clouds.

She stared back at Noah. "I'm not copying. I've got my own idea."

"Right."

"I have. Anyway, why don't you stop spying on me and get on with your mud bath."

"It's not a mud bath." Noah looked back

toward his yard. "And I'm not spying. I've got my own idea, too. Better than yours."

"Sure." Abby peered over the fence. Noah's mud bath was a mess. Someone had dug chunks out of the sides with a plastic spade. Next to it was a pink plate in the shape of a flower, with mud pies piled higgledy-piggledy on top.

"That's not it," said Noah. "It's . . ." He pointed down the side of his house, near the water tank.

The grass was long there, and all Abby could see was the handle of a shovel and what looked like some old bags lying around.

"It's what?"

"Never mind." Noah scrambled down from the tree. "You dig your hole, and I'll dig mine."

"Good idea."

Abby watched him walk back toward the water tank, past the mud bath and the rusty swing set and the jungle of weeds. Everything at his place was old and broken and falling down.

She knew Max wouldn't like it there.

She knew he would rather be at her house.

So she dug every day.

Noah did, too.

Sometimes Abby watched him over the fence. She saw his head bob up and down as he dug. She heard him yell as he tripped over a rusty old tricycle. She heard the sound of water running.

Every day, she dug deeper and faster.

And every morning, she held her breath.

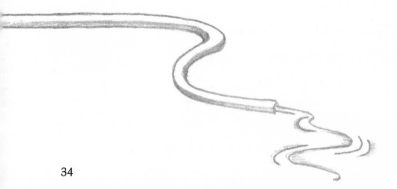

Cloudy, with a Chance of Ducks

Abby lay on the trampoline and stared up at the clouds. She imagined Max sitting here next to her, quacking softly, his fat little body bobbing up and down.

Then she sighed. It was turning out to be hard, getting Max. It was turning out to be harder than she had ever imagined.

Every morning, kids lined up at Mrs. Melvino's desk.

Every morning, Mrs. Melvino shook her head and said, "Oh dear, no."

Every day, she told them more about Max's demands.

She said even if you drained your swimming pool and filled it up with fresh, clean water, it still wouldn't do.

"It's too big. Max needs something a little more . . . cozy."

She said even if you put a plastic Batman mask over your ferret's face, it was still considered "toothy."

She said Max was not interested in strawberry-flavored candies.

She said for a yard to be *secure,* the gate needed a lock.

"Max will not *fly* away. But he has a very clever beak. And he will wander, if you let him. In search of strawberries, most likely."

Finally, she said it wasn't enough to *tell* her about your clean aquatic environment and your mud bath and your nice secure yard.

"I must have *proof.* Photographs. Diagrams. Maybe a sample of the water, just to be safe."

Abby sighed. Every day, Max got more demanding.

Still, he was going to be worth it.

Everything was more fun with Max in class.

He waddled around, quacking and flapping and making people draw green volcanoes.

Mrs. Melvino never freaked out about the mess or the noise, or anything at all.

She just clicked her tongue and smiled, giving Max her special sideways look.

She said the water would dry and the mess could be cleaned up, and if Max should happen to open the craft cupboard with his very clever beak, spilling markers and paints and rolls of paper everywhere, well, then, that must mean it was time to do some crafts.

"Thank you, Max!" she said. "What an excellent idea."

Sometimes if Max quacked loudly enough, Mrs. Melvino canceled their spelling test and read them a book instead. Max sat on the mat, with his head cocked to one side as if he was listening.

Sometimes after lunch they went outside to sit under the trees. "Ducks need fresh air!"

said Mrs. Melvino. "They need grass. And sky."

They lay on their backs and looked for shapes in the clouds.

Somehow, every shape Mrs. Melvino found looked strangely like a duck.

After a while the clouds above Abby's trampoline had started to look like ducks, too.

Abby shaded her eyes with one hand and squinted up at the sky.

Today there was one that looked a bit like a beak, if you tilted your head at just the right angle.

Abby sat up.

Maybe she should take photos of the clouds, too, just in case?

She had photos of everything else now— of her big bag of pellets and her strawberries and her calm, secure yard. Of her built-in, dug-in aquatic environment with a mud bath on the side.

She was finally finished.

Her holes were big enough. She had slid her clamshells inside. She had filled them up with clean water. She had scooped up some dirt and added it to one half. Not too much, not too little. Just enough for a perfect duck-friendly mud bath.

She had arranged her photos into a folder with little plastic pockets. She had used colored sticky notes to divide it into sections. Each one had a curly-writing heading—*calm, secure, aquatic, muddy*—and each photo had a label—*pellets, gate, mud.*

Now she would add just one more:

Duck-shaped clouds

She picked up the camera.

Click. Click. Click.

Then she lay back on the trampoline and smiled.

Tomorrow was the day.

The Duck Speaks

"Well," said Mrs. Melvino. "This is excellent."

Abby jiggled on the balls of her feet.

In front of her, Noah was beaming.

Abby leaned forward, trying to sneak a peek at the diagrams and plans he had spread out on the desk.

She couldn't believe it.

She had gotten here earlier than anyone ever came to school. Before the crossing guard put his flags out. Before the sprinklers came on.

But when she came around the corner, Noah was waiting outside the classroom. His bag was zipped up, and his shoelaces were tied.

There were no toast crumbs around his mouth.

Abby stared at him.
He must have skipped
breakfast. He must
have gotten up and
grabbed his stuff
and run straight
out the door.

She should tell
Mrs. Melvino.

It was important
to eat breakfast.
That's what Mom
said. It wasn't fair
for her to lose Max
because she had been delayed by Cheerios.

"Excellent." Mrs. Melvino peered at the
screen of Noah's camera. "Though it would
be easier if you printed these out. It's hard to
see . . . Good heavens, what is that? It looks
like a . . . leg?"

"Nothing." Noah jabbed at a button.

"Oh! Is that a *head*?"

Noah sighed. "It's . . . a Barbie. My sisters were playing pool party."

"Pool party?" Mrs. Melvino shook her head. "Oh dear, no. Max cannot share his pond with *Barbies*."

"I'll take it out." Noah pushed another button. "I just forgot before."

"Yes." Mrs. Melvino nodded. "Then take some new photos. And print them out this time so I can get a proper look."

"I can't," Noah began. "I—"

"I printed mine," Abby said quickly. "Here."

"Goodness." Mrs. Melvino reached for Abby's folder. She flipped through, peering at each photo in turn. "This is very impressive."

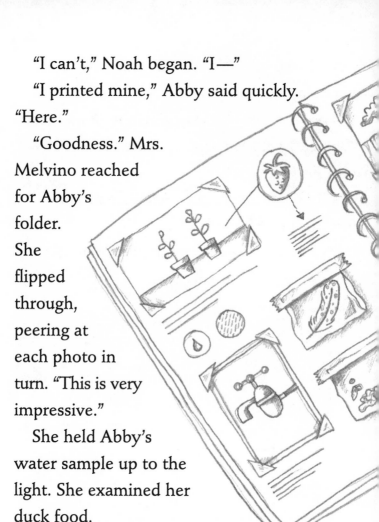

She held Abby's water sample up to the light. She examined her duck food.

"Well," she said, "you certainly seem to have everything."

Abby's heart raced.

She was about to get Max. She knew it.

Mrs. Melvino snapped the folder shut, then frowned. "Still, I'm not sure. It's difficult to find a good day. Max has a very busy schedule." She opened her planner. "Tomorrow is Wednesday—that's pizza night. Thursdays we watch cartoons." She turned some pages. "And next week is going to be hot. Do you have air-conditioning? Perhaps a portable fan? Max is *very* sensitive to heat." She jabbed a finger at the folder. "I don't suppose there's a photo of a fan in here?"

Abby shook her head. "I didn't—"

"Oh." Mrs. Melvino reached out to stroke Max's feathers. "Well, I don't know."

"QUACK!" Max flapped his wings, shaking off Mrs. Melvino's hand. He nudged the planner with his beak, flipping some pages over. Then he waddled across until he was standing next to it. Then on the edge of it. Then right on top of it.

On Tuesday.

Today.

He nestled his feathery bottom down right on top of today. Then he tilted his head and gave Mrs. Melvino a kind of sideways look.

"Today!" said Abby.

Mrs. Melvino turned white. "Today? Oh, I don't think—"

"It's not pizza night. Or cartoons. Or too hot."

"Oh dear," said Mrs. Melvino. "Oh—"

"QUACK!" said Max.

"Well." Mrs. Melvino nodded slowly. "It looks like the duck has spoken."

Duck Sleepover

Abby lay on her back and stared up at the clouds.

Next to her, Max bobbed up and down, quacking softly as the trampoline bounced underneath him.

Every now and then, he hopped down for a swim in the pond or to play in the mud bath.

Abby let Max eat some pellets out of her hand. Then she gave him a strawberry.

When she heard Noah on the other side of the fence, she sighed. She knew it wouldn't be long before he scrambled up the tree and started staring at her.

But he didn't.

He stayed on his side all afternoon, poking around down by the water tank. Sometimes

Abby heard the sound of water running or Noah whispering to one of his sisters.

A couple of times, she heard a door slamming and someone yelling inside the house.

At dinnertime Abby gave Max another strawberry, then closed the sliding door behind her.

While they ate, Max stood with his beak pressed up against the glass.

"Couldn't we—?" Abby began.

"Absolutely not," said Dad. "He's a *duck,* Abby, not a dinner guest."

Dad pulled the curtains across so Max couldn't see in anymore. Instead, Max started tapping on the glass. He tapped softly at first, as if to say, *Hey, I think you've forgotten me,* and then more loudly, as if to say, *Let me in, or else!*

After a while, it was so loud that Mom started looking like she needed to sit down on the sofa with a nice cup of tea.

"All right," Dad said finally, "as long as he's quiet."

At bedtime Abby settled Max down in his cage in the laundry room. The straw wasn't as good as a duvet, but it would have to do.

Mom said Max most definitely could not sleep on Abby's bed.

"It's a duck visit," she said. "Not a sleepover."

A duck sleepover. Abby liked the sound of that.

Maybe when Mrs. Melvino saw how well she had looked after Max, she would let him come again.

Maybe when Mom and Dad saw how clean and well behaved he was, they would let him sleep on her feet.

Maybe if she promised to get pizza, he could stay tomorrow night, too.

Good Morning, Duck

In the morning, Abby hurried down to the laundry room.

Then she stopped.

Max wasn't in his cage.

That was okay, though, because he was probably in the kitchen, sitting up at the table, hoping for waffles.

But he wasn't in the kitchen. And the sliding door was open.

Abby's heart raced as she remembered his very clever beak.

That was okay, though, because he was probably in the yard.

He had to be in the yard, because it was secure. It had a nice high fence and a gate with a lock.

She changed
quickly into her
uniform, then ran
outside.

But Max wasn't in
the yard. He wasn't in
the pond or on the
trampoline or behind the shed.

"Max!" she called.

She waited for a rustling in
the grass or the sound
of soft, padding feet.

But there was
nothing.

Abby looked
around her.
Where could he be?

She knew he
couldn't fly.

Mrs. Melvino said he could only
do short hops, just a few feet at
a time, just a few . . .

Abby froze. She looked at the bag of pellets and the trampoline and the fence.

One little hop onto the bag. One little hop onto the trampoline. One little hop to the fence. One little hop to the tree.

She raced to the fence and looked over. What if Noah had stolen Max? What if at this very moment Max was curled up on Noah's duvet?

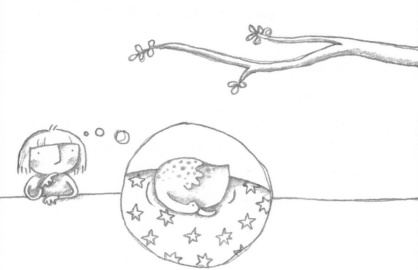

Noah's mother would let him sleep there. Abby knew it. She didn't care about messes or noise or duck sleepovers. Not like Mom, who was always frowning and saying, "That place is a crazy madhouse! Can you imagine?"

Abby swung up into the tree, then dropped down into Noah's yard and hurried toward the house.

When she got to the water tank, she stopped.

There in the long grass was a pond.

It was round and wide and deep. It was built-in and not at all muddy.

It was lined with what looked like real cement.

It was really very aquatic.

The water was weird, though. It wasn't muddy or clean; it was a strange pink color.

There was something in there, too, floating on the surface.

Something green and small.

Strawberry leaves.

Lots of them.

And a duck feather, smooth and brown.

Abby looked frantically around her.

Max wasn't in the pond. He wasn't anywhere in the yard. There was just long grass and dirt and a couple of old bikes leaning up against the fence.

The front fence. With its lock and its bolt and its gate.

Its gate swinging open.

Abby ran through the yard and the open gate and out onto the street, looking around her wildly. Left. Right. Straight ahead.

Which way would she go if she was a duck?

Then she saw them, on the sidewalk in front of her.

Footprints.

Duckprints.

Left. Max had gone left.

Left meant the shops up the road. It meant traffic and parking lots. It meant the pet shop with its clawed and toothy animals.

Abby ran.

One Particular Duck

Abby raced along the sidewalk following the duckprints.

Cars sped past, and her heart thumped. Would a clever duck know the difference between a sidewalk and a road?

She kept running . . .

past the building site with its piles of bricks and tiles . . .

past the vacant lot with the graffiti on the fence . . .

past the corner house with the loud, fence-rattling bulldog . . .

and all the way to the shopping center.

The man who owned the pet shop was out front. He was setting out cages and bowls of food for toothy little puppies.

"Excuse me!" Abby said, panting. "Have you seen a duck?"

The man shook his head. "We don't sell ducks, love. How about a puppy?" He pointed to the window. "Chihuahuas are very popular right now. Portable, too."

Abby shook her head. "I'm looking for a duck."

"Can't help you there." The man turned to go inside, then stopped. "You could try the park, of course."

The park?

Abby stared at him.

Where would she go if she was a duck?

Of course.

She ran faster this time. It was getting late. It was time to be eating breakfast and packing her schoolbag. It was time to be putting Max in his nice, secure cage with some pellets and maybe a strawberry or two.

It was time to be handing him safely back to Mrs. Melvino.

She had to get Max back. She had to get him safely into his cage, into the car, into the classroom.

She couldn't tell Mrs. Melvino she had lost him. She just couldn't.

Maybe Melanie had been right all along. Maybe it was sensible to keep your pet in a bag.

That way it couldn't escape and waddle three dangerous blocks past traffic and bulldogs and toothy little puppies.

Abby looked down at the sidewalk.

The duckprints were so faint now, they were almost invisible.

When she reached the park, they disappeared completely.

It didn't matter, though. She didn't need duckprints to tell her where to go.

Not anymore.

She ran through the park, past the swings and the slide, over the hill, and all the way down the grass, toward the biggest, most natural, built-in aquatic environment a duck could ever wish for.

The lake.

There were ducks out on the water, the same as always. Mother ducks and baby ducks and somewhere-in-between ducks, all swimming and splashing and diving about.

But one particular duck stood out.

One particular duck with a particularly smooth orange beak and particularly speckled brown feathers.

Abby stood at the very edge, where the ground was wet and soft. "MAX!" she called. "MAX!"

Max turned. He flapped his wings and quacked softly.

But he didn't move. He just sat there, bobbing up and down, up and down on the water.

Because he didn't come if you called him. He wasn't that kind of pet.

Abby looked out at the lake. It must be deep all the way out there.

It was definitely cold. And wet. And kind of slimy.

There was a sign nearby that said NO SWIMMING.

She supposed that didn't apply to ducks.

"Come on, Max."

She said it softly to herself, as if she wasn't calling him.

But Max just sat there, staring.

Abby's heart sank. She would

have to go back. She would have to run all the way home and tell Mom and Dad about Max. She would have to watch them shake their heads and say, *See, I told you pets are too much trouble!* and *All that quacking and flapping, all that tapping on the glass, all this fuss and drama on a school day!*

She would never have a kind-of-sort-of pet for a day again.

Her stomach twisted. She couldn't leave Max here. But she couldn't stay with him either. Mom and Dad would be looking for her. They would be calling and frowning and wondering if it was time to start freaking out.

It probably was.

Then Abby heard a sound.

Footsteps, coming down the hill behind her.

The Duck Is a Dream

"Hey! Abby!"

Abby turned. She knew that voice. It was different, though. It was loud and strong and not at all soft or creepy.

"Where is he?" Noah puffed to a stop beside her.

Abby pointed. "I think he went over the fence. He . . ."

"Yeah, I heard him. He went QUACK outside my window."

Abby frowned. "Why didn't you stop him?"

"I was half asleep. I thought it was a dream. Then I heard you later, going out the gate." Noah turned to Abby. "How did you find him?"

Abby told him about the duckprints and the

pink water, and he nodded. "Food coloring. My sisters said Barbie needed a pink pool." He sighed. "They're always getting into my stuff. They ate my strawberries, so I had to buy more. That's why . . ."

"What?"

"That's why I couldn't print the photos. I ran out of money."

"Oh."

Noah nodded toward the lake. "What are you going to do?"

"I don't know." Abby sat down on the grass and stared out at the water.

"I could go in if you want." Noah inched toward the edge.

Abby pointed to the sign. "It says no swimming. Anyway, you'd get all wet. You'd . . . wait, are those your *pajamas*?"

She stared at Noah. His feet were bare, and he was wearing fuzzy brown pants and a tattered old shirt.

Noah flushed. "Yeah, I kind of left in a

hurry." He looked down at his shirt. "It's old. I don't care if it gets wet."

Before Abby could stop him, he stepped off the edge and started wading through the ankle-deep water, through the mud.

"Careful!" she said. "It's . . ."

"Muddy?" Noah lifted one slime-covered foot. "Yeah, I know."

Abby looked out at the ducks. They seemed closer, somehow. They *were* closer. In fact, they were swimming quickly toward them, the way they did when she and Mom used to bring stale bread down. "They think you're going to feed them!" She jumped to her feet. "Have you got anything?"

"In my pajamas?" Noah stuck his hands in his pockets. "Umm, there's a bit of fluff here."

"Just pretend! Hold it out."

Noah staggered toward the ducks through the slippery mud. In one hand, he held out a disgusting-looking ball of pocket fluff. With the other, he fought to keep his balance as he stumbled deeper and deeper, up to his knees now in the dark water.

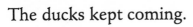

The ducks kept coming.

Abby leaned forward. Where was Max?
He must be in there somewhere.

"I see him!" Noah yelled.

"Where?" Suddenly, it was one big
blur of ducks, all of them flapping
and splashing and pecking at
each other, all trying to be
first to reach Noah's gross
pile of fluff.

"There!" Noah pointed
with his free hand.

The one he was using
to balance.

Then he slipped
forward, into the ducks.

Feathers and fluff went
flying.

And Noah went under
with a splash.

Duck Out of Reach

Abby looked frantically around her.

There was a man walking his dog over by the swings. There was a woman jogging along the path up near the road.

They were too far away.

She turned back to the lake.

Noah was coming up and coughing, then waving his arms and sinking again.

Abby looked down at her uniform. It was freshly washed and neatly ironed.

Suddenly, she wished she had worn her pajamas.

She took a step toward the edge, then stopped.

Out on the lake, there was quacking and flapping and splashing and coughing. There were hands and feet and feathers flying as the ducks fought over the fluff, pecking and pulling it from beak to beak.

She couldn't go out into the middle of that. She would end up coughing and waving and sinking just like Noah.

She looked around her again.

In swimming class, the teacher always had something you could hold out. Something long and thin you could reach out toward your friend and haul them in safely. Something like a pool noodle or a broomstick or maybe even . . . a tree branch! Like the one lying over there on the grass.

Abby ran and grabbed it. It was heavier than a noodle and more splintery than a broomstick, but it was long and thin and really exactly the perfect kind of thing to reach out toward your friend . . . toward Noah . . . when he was coughing and waving and sinking in a lake.

She took a deep breath and stepped into the mud.

It was squelchy and squishy. It sucked at her feet.

She stumbled toward the ducks and held out the branch. "Grab on!"

Noah did. His hands wrapped around it, and she pulled him up.

He was wet and slimy, but he was okay.

"Thanks!" Noah wiped a string of lake weed from his face. "It's not actually that deep, is it?"

"Not really."

He flushed. "I guess I kind of panicked. The ducks . . . the beaks . . . you know?"

"Yeah." Abby looked around. The ducks had shooed. They had flapped and flown and swum away.

All except one.

One particular duck with a particularly smooth orange beak and particularly speckled brown feathers.

Max was bobbing up and down just a little distance away, just out of reach.

Noah looked at Abby. "He's not going to come, is he?"

She shook her head.

Noah sighed. "You stay here and watch him. I'd better go and get Mrs. Melvino."

Abby stared at Noah, at his dripping pajamas and the green lake weed strung through his hair. "Like that?"

Noah shrugged. "Everyone thinks I'm a weirdo, anyway."

Abby didn't reply. Maybe Noah was right. Not about the weirdo thing. Well, maybe about that, too. But also about Mrs. Melvino. It was getting late. She would be at school by now, marking spelling tests and practicing her curly writing.

She would come if Noah told her.

She would come running, with her skirt flying and her earrings jingling.

She would know exactly what to do. She would click her tongue and look at Max sideways, and he would swim right over to her.

And Abby would be glad, because Max
was safe, because he had made it past traffic
and toothy animals, and out of the deep, cold,
slimy lake.

But she would be sad, too.

Because she would know she was never
getting Max again, no matter how much pizza
she bought.

Abby looked at Noah. Suddenly she knew
just what to do. "Wait. I think I have a better
idea."

Duck on the Move

Abby clicked her tongue and looked sideways.

From the middle of the lake, Max stared back at her.

He didn't move.

"Wiggle your eyebrows!" said Noah.

Abby wiggled.

Max kept staring.

"Wiggle harder!" said Noah.

Abby shook her head. She stopped wiggling. And thought. She tried to remember how Mrs. Melvino did it.

She peered out at Max the way Mrs. Melvino peered over her glasses. She clicked more softly and tilted her head farther. She swished her skirt a little and shook her head.

If she had earrings, they would be jingling.

She was sure of it.

Slowly, Max started to move. Then more quickly, his duck bottom gliding smoothly over the surface of the water.

"He's coming!" said Noah.

"Shhh!" said Abby. "Pretend you don't care."

Max swam toward them. Soon Abby could see his little feet paddling under the water. He was almost here. Just a little farther and she would have him. Just a little . . .

"Abby!"

"Noah!"

Suddenly, there were voices yelling. And footsteps coming down the hill.

"It's your mom," said Noah. "And my mom. And my sisters."

Abby didn't turn her head. She kept on clicking and swishing and jingling. Because Max was right here now. He was bobbing up and down in front of her, waiting.

She leaned forward and scooped him up. *Safe*.

She held him tightly in both arms and squelched back through the mud.

Mom's face was white. Then red. Then a strange kind of purple.

"What are you *doing*, Abby?" she said. "We've been looking everywhere!"

She had looked out back, she said. Then out front. Then around the corner, where she had run into Noah's mother.

Noah's mother turned to Abby. "I thought you might have gone to school early. Your dad went to check."

"Then the pet shop man said you might be here," Mom went on, "but I thought he meant the park, not the lake, not the *water* . . . Oh, just look at your *uniform*!"

"You, too, Noah," his mother said, but her mouth was curved in a kind-of-sort-of smile. "Wow. I didn't think that shirt could look any worse!"

"We had to," Abby began. "He wouldn't come. He—"

Then she stopped because there were more footsteps now. There was someone else coming over the top of the hill, another voice yelling.

"MAX!"

Mrs. Melvino flew toward them, skirt flapping, earrings jingling. Dad stumbled after her, puffing and panting.

She raced down the hill, her curly hair bouncing.

She didn't slow down when she got to the bottom. She didn't seem to see Abby or Noah. She just kept running, her eyes fixed on the middle of the lake.

She ran right past them and jumped into the water.

"Don't panic! I'll get him!" Her feet sank into the mud, and her skirt floated out around her. "MAX!"

"I've got him," Abby said softly. "He's here."

"What?" Mrs. Melvino whirled around. Her face softened when she saw Max snuggled in Abby's arms. "But how did he . . . I mean, how did you . . . ?"

"I'm sorry," said Abby. "It was—"

The fence, she was going to say. *The strawberries. Just a few short hops . . .*

"It was my fault," Noah said quickly. "I left the gate open. I—"

"No, no!" Mrs. Melvino waded back out onto the grass and reached out for Max. "I mean, how did you get him out of the lake? Strawberries, I suppose? Good thinking! I always carry an emergency supply, just in case."

Abby shook her head. "It wasn't strawberries. I—"

"She clicked!" said Noah. "Like this. And . . ." He tilted his head and fixed Mrs. Melvino with a very Melvino-ish stare.

"Goodness! Well, yes, I suppose that would work. That's rather clever, actually." Mrs. Melvino smiled at Dad. "What a sensible child you have. You must be very proud."

Dad nodded but didn't reply. He was bent over, trying to catch his breath.

"But how did you know we were here?" said Mom. "I was just about to call."

Mrs. Melvino turned to Dad. "Once I heard Max was gone . . . well . . . where else would he be? Where would you go if you were a duck?" She turned to Abby. "I should have warned you. He does like swimming. Still, you'll know for next time. Do bring some strawberries, though. It's much easier on the neck than all that tilting and staring."

Abby nodded. "Okay," she said. "I—"

Then she stopped. Because all of a sudden she realized what Mrs. Melvino had said.

She had said *clever* and *sensible* and *you must be very proud*. And they were good things, all of them.

But she had said something else, too. Something even better.

Next time.

She had said *next time.*

A Few Small Hops

"Really?" Abby looked up at Mrs. Melvino.

Mrs. Melvino nodded. "You've taken such good care of him."

"But he got out," Abby said. "The yard wasn't secure."

Mrs. Melvino sighed. "Yes, well. He does get out. A lot. He has a very clever beak, you know." She smiled. "But you rescued him. You went into the lake."

Mom groaned. "Yes, in your uniform!"

"Oh, don't worry about that!" Mrs. Melvino waved a hand. "It's only water. And a bit of slime. And"—she peered at Abby's shirt—"what's that gray stuff?"

"Pocket fluff," said Noah.

"Ah. Of course. I'm sure it will wash out."

"Really?" Mom stared doubtfully at the shirt. "I don't think . . ."

Noah's mother nodded. "Oh, yes. Trust me. I've had a lot of practice with pocket fluff. Mud, too." She shot a glance at Noah's sisters, who giggled. Then she turned to Mom. "I could help you if you want, show you some of my tricks."

"Oh." Mom hesitated. She looked from Noah to his mother and back again. Then she nodded

slowly. "Well, why not? That's very kind of you. Isn't it, Abby?"

Abby smiled back at Mom. But she didn't say anything. She was too busy thinking about Max. About *next time.*

She could move the trampoline so he couldn't escape. She could bring him to the lake herself. She could stuff emergency strawberries in her pockets and walk with him, all the way there, then all the way home again.

Maybe Noah could come, too? They could watch Max together. They could take turns carrying him home.

Or . . . ?

She looked across at Noah, in his bare feet and his pajamas. She thought about his pink pond and his sisters and how he had gone into the lake and under the water.

"I think Noah should have him," she said. "He's got cement. And strawberries."

"Really?" said Mrs. Melvino.

But Noah shook his head. "I . . . ran out of strawberries. And I haven't got photos."

"You could use our printer," Abby said. "If you want. I've got some strawberries left, too."

Noah stared at her. "Could I?"

Mrs. Melvino frowned. "Actually," she said, "I've been thinking about the demands. I suspect they might be a bit too . . . demanding. I also suspect that perhaps they are *my* demands rather than Max's. Today he has swum in lake water and slimy mud. He has waddled over fences and through traffic." She set Max down on the grass in front of her and smiled. "And he is fine. In fact, he has never seemed better."

She turned to Noah. "So, how about tonight?"

"Tonight?" Noah's eyes grew wide. "For Max?"

Mrs. Melvino nodded.

"But . . . what about pizza night?"

Mrs. Melvino laughed. "Oh, I suspect Max will manage without pizza for one night. I really only let him eat the anchovies, anyway. Pizza is very bad for ducks, you know."

Abby saw a slow smile creep across Noah's face. She saw him click his tongue and give Max a secret sideways look.

Then she grinned. Tonight Max would be just over the fence.

If she sat on the trampoline, she might hear him quacking.

If she peeked through the fence, she might see him splashing in Noah's pink pond.

"Hey." Noah turned to her. "Maybe . . . do you want to come over? You could help keep my sisters out of the way."

"To your place?" Abby hesitated. She imagined herself in Noah's crazy madhouse with the long grass and the piles of junk and the hundred lost tennis balls, with the sisters and the Barbies and the disgusting gray pocket fluff.

Then she smiled. Yes. She could do that.
She could climb from the trampoline to the
long branch and down the
tree. She would be on
Noah's side before she
knew it.

It was just a few
small hops, after all.